JFG
VOL 2/2

MORE TORTOISE TALES

More Tortoise Tales

Sheila Groves

VICTORY PRESS

EASTBOURNE

ISBN 0 85476 247 7

Text and cover illustrations
by Diane Matthes

Printed in Great Britain for
VICTORY PRESS (Evangelical Publishers Ltd)
Lottbridge Drove, Eastbourne, E. Sussex BN23 6NT
by Fletcher & Son Ltd. Norwich

CONTENTS

1

Leapalong and Back Again

Take-Your-Time shambled happily up to his great-grandpapa.

"Great-grandpapa," he announced excitedly, not waiting to discover which end of the elderly tortoise was which, "I'm going to school now, and I can almost read!"

More-Haste-Less-Speed's head emerged slowly from the opposite end of his shell. "It's a pity they don't teach you manners as well," he remarked gruffly. "Hardly shut my eyes!"

"Sorry, great-grandpapa," but Take-Your-Time was too excited to be really sorry. "Can I show you, great-grandpapa?"

More-Haste-Less-Speed blinked once or twice to shake the sleep from his eyes and reached for his big bunch of keys. Unlocking the little door in the bumpiest part of his shell, he pulled out a greenish leaf mottled with yellow and handed it to his great-grandson.

"Here you are, then - see what you can make of that!"

Take-Your-Time took it eagerly, decided which way up it should go, and studied the first line.

"In the dark green pond at the bottom of the field," he began slowly, "lived a family of frogs called Leapalong. They were a happy family, mother and father, Croakus and Lenny. But one day Lenny decided that the pond was too small: he wanted to see the world! He wanted to go on an - an - great-greatpapa, what's that word?"

More-Haste-Less-Speed peered over his shoulder. "Expedition; that's a long journey," he added. "Yes, you're coming on nicely, my lad; but perhaps you'd better let me finish the story now, or we'll be here until Midsummer's Eve!"

Lenny wanted to go on an expedition, so he plucked up his courage and went to tell his father. At first his father was quite upset; "Do you mean you're not happy here, son?"

"Well, not exactly," Lenny fidgeted and looked for the right words. "But there must be so many more things outside this pond, just waiting to be discovered - and I want to go and discover them!"

His father sighed. "Well, remember all the things your mother and I have taught you since you were a tiny tadpole, and promise me you'll not do anything silly!"

"Yes, yes!" Lenny was eager to be off. "And can I - can I have some money, please father?"

Father Leapalong unlocked a little drawer in his corner cupboard and pulled out something wrapped in a waterlily leaf.

"Don't spend it all at once," he handed it to Lenny. "And take care!"

Lenny said goodbye to his mother (Croakus was sulking

under some duckweed in the far corner of the pond), gave an enormous hop right out of the pond and landed on the bank. The world was his to explore!

Crossing a field a few days later he came to a gap in the hedge; just as he was about to pass through, a rabbit appeared from nowhere and, holding out his paw, said "Private way! 5p please!" 5p! Lenny was horrified but he didn't like to argue, so he delved into his waterlily leaf and produced 5p, passed hastily

through and hurried down a path between golden stalks of corn. After several days he came to a little wood. On the edge of the wood he found a notice which said 'Tonight! Gala performance: singing, dancing, food. All welcome. 20p.''

"That's more like it," thought Lenny, following the directions on the notice.

He soon met a weasel - very

friendly - who offered to take him on a guided tour of the wood first, for only 10p. Everyone wanted to be his friend, and Lenny really began to enjoy himself. The only trouble was, everything cost so much money.

He stayed in the wood for several days: always there were new friends to meet and entertainments provided; Lenny was so glad he'd left his dark green, boring little pond far behind.

But one day when he reached into his waterlilly leaf, he found his money had nearly all gone.

"Oh dear!" he thought. "Tomorrow I must try to find some work."

But tomorrow there was a grand entertainment put on by the stoats and weasels, and they'd asked Lenny to do a special trampoline act. . . so tomorrow came and went, and Lenny had even less money in his waterlily leaf, and no work.

And finally the day came when Lenny opened his waterlily leaf and found nothing in it at all.

It was two days since he had eaten anything, but somehow none of his friends seemed interested any more. Eventually he managed to sell his new green coat to a lizard in exchange for a very stingy breakfast, and set off to look for work. But it seemed that the wood was full of people with no work.

"No," said the badger abruptly. "Nothing for the likes of you."

"Sorry," said a tired-looking squirrel. "You're the fifteenth person this morning."

"Work?" the owl hooted with laughter. "You must be joking!"

Just as he was about to give up, he met an elderly toad.

"Can you swim?" enquired the toad, looking him up and down.

Lenny ignored the question. "Got a young 'un who missed out on his schooling - backward he is; I'll feed you if you can teach him to swim, but I can't pay you."

Lenny struggled with himself. The toad was old and dirty and smelt of stagnant water. But what else could he do? "I'll come," he said briefly, and followed the toad to a pool of the darkest foulest water he'd ever come upon.

"Make yourself at home," the toad invited him, and went to fetch his young 'un.

The next few days were the most wretched Lenny had ever spent. He lived on nothing but stale duckweed, and had nothing to do all day except teach young 'un to swim - and young 'un was not only stupid but extremely rude.

"Fancy a Leapalong ending up like this!" he thought. "If my father could see me now!" And at the thought of his kind old father, two large tears welled up and splashed into the thick, still water. Finally he made up his mind. "I've had enough of adventuring," he said to the old toad. "I'm going home!" The old toad shrugged and turned away.

The nearer he came to his dark green pond, the slower Lenny went. Whatever would his father say? He was still quite a way away when he suddenly saw someone leaping through the grass to meet him.

"Father!" Lenny couldn't

believe his eyes.

"Lenny, my boy! Good to see you," his father held out his arms.

Lenny hesitated. "Father, I've wasted all your money and got myself into some horrible muddles. I'm sorry, really I am; I've come back to work for you - I don't deserve to be a Leapalong any more," and he hung his head in shame.

But his father took him into his arms and hugged him and, before he could protest any more, he took him home and gave him a new coat and an enormous supper.

But Croakus went and sulked under the duckweed. . .

"And you'd better be gone," More-Haste-Less-Speed looked at his great-grandson over the top of his spectacles, "or your mother will think you've gone on an

expedition too!"

Take-Your-Time nodded. "Yes, great-grandpapa. Lenny was lucky, wasn't he?"

"Lucky?" said his great-grandpapa. "All depends who your father is."

Lenny did lots of things that were silly and wrong: sometimes he didn't know any better, but sometimes he did. But in the end he did something sensible: what was that?

Jesus told a story like this one, about a man with two sons; you can read it in Luke's gospel, chapter 15. Jesus told it to show that we all do things that are silly and wrong and, when we do, we must come back to God, our

Father, and tell him we're sorry. If we do, he will forgive us and let us start again, because he is a loving Father who will always welcome us back.

Can you think of things now which were wrong and make you feel far away from God? He isn't really far away; he's just waiting to know that you are sorry.

2

Waiting for Willoughby

There wasn't a cloud in the sky when Take-Your-Time left home for his great-grandpapa's syca-more tree, but he was no more than half way there when there was a sudden flash, followed by a low rumbling noise, and a second later the clouds opened and the rain just emptied down.

Patter, patter, patter, it went on Take-Your-Time's shell. Drip, drip, splash! it went off the end of his nose.

And by the time he arrived at More-Haste-Less-Speed's front

door, he was a very wet little tortoise indeed.

"Tut, tut! Mind the bedding," his great-grandpapa steered him round the pile of dry leaves in the corner. "Came without your umbrella-leaf, did you?"

"But it was all sunny when I left, great-grandpapa - a-a-choo!"

"Ah, but you must be ready for anything, my lad - never know what might happen! Here, dry your feet and hand me my keys."

And while Take-Your-Time rubbed his feet with a rough nettle-leaf towel, More-Haste-Less-Speed unfolded a small brown story, slightly chewed at the edges, and began:

Everywhere you looked there were mice: mice in the coal scuttle, mice on the bed; mice on

the kitchen dresser and up in the
attic; mice in the cellar and
swinging from the chandeliers.
And they were all Getting Ready.
You've never seen such a dusting
and sweeping, such a making of
beds, such a stocking of larders:
and all because Cousin Willoughby of Double Gloucester was
coming back.

All the mice, even Twitchit, the tiniest of them all, had heard about Cousin Willoughby. Adventures? Cousin Willoughby had had them all; daring and heroic deeds? Cousin Willoughby had lost count of how many he'd done; and he was said to be the most handsome, kind and generous mouse that anyone had ever known. And he was coming back!

"When is Cousin Willoughby coming?" asked Twitchit, scuttling out of the way of the dusters.

"This week - next week - who knows?" Whiskers polished away at the chandelier for all he was worth. "We just know he's coming, that's all - and we must be ready for him! Now, run along and play, Twitchit, and stop getting in the way!"

Three days later everything was spick and span: not a speck of dust, not a crumb of cheese to be seen anywhere. The mice paused for a while; since there was no sign of Cousin Willoughby, they worked out a rota of dusting and polishing to keep everything ready for when he finally arrived.

No one knew who first started the rumours. Perhaps it was Sidle; he was always causing trouble. But there it was, whispering from ear to ear: "Cousin Willoughby's not *really* coming - it's just a story!"

Some of the mice, like Whiskers, were indignant. "Of course he's coming," they said. "He said he would, didn't he? Don't you believe him?"

But others were only too pleased to believe the whispers, because it meant they could stop scrubbing and polishing and mending.

Soon Whiskers and his friends found they couldn't possibly keep everywhere clean by themselves; "Never mind," Whiskers told them. "We'll just keep our part tidy; at least there'll be somewhere ready for Cousin Willoughby!"

Sidle crept up beside him and cleared his throat. "Ahem! Have you ever *seen* Cousin Willoughby, Whiskers?"

"Of course not," said Whiskers. "He was off adventuring before I was born! None of us has seen him, you know that."

"Mmm," Sidle looked thoughtful. "Well, I don't believe there *is* a Cousin Willoughby at all!"

Whiskers was shocked. "But we've all heard about him," he said. "Our fathers knew him! And it talks about him in The Books."

Sidle shrugged. "You believe what you like," he said. "If you want to spend your life slaving away with brooms and dusters and polish, carry on! I'm going to enjoy myself!"

And, as Cousin Willoughby still didn't come, one by one all the other mice decided to enjoy themselves too, and soon everywhere was littered with cheese rind, lollipop sticks and unwashed milk

bottles, and the mice spent most of their time sleeping, scavenging and quarrelling.

Only Whiskers and baby Twitchit still believed that Cousin Willoughby would come back and still kept their tiny corner of the hole as neat as a new pin. But at times even they began to be miserable, because no one else would speak to them, and they wondered whether Cousin Willoughby would ever come.

29

Whiskers was getting old and stiff and one day, when it was very cold and wet, Twitchit had made him up a neat little bed out of old matchboxes and cotton wool. He was just going to hunt for some cream for Whiskers' poor stiff paws, when there was a great commotion outside, followed by a loud knock on the door. Twitchit scuttled to open it.

Outside, splendid in red velvet and gold braid and followed by a whole troupe of friends and relations, stood Cousin Willoughby. For a moment Twitchit was too overcome to speak; then he remembered his manners.

"Won't you come in?" He held the door politely. "We've - er - tried to keep everything ready for you, but I'm afraid you may find things rather cramped." And he led the way to Whiskers' neat, but pitifully small corner.

Cousin Willoughby could see at once what had happened; he gazed at the unwashed milk bottles, the cheese rind, the lollipop sticks and spiders' webs everwhere except in Whiskers' corner - and noticed that all the other mice seemed suddenly to have disappeared.

"Yes," he said quietly, with a smile for Whiskers. "It's very nice and comfortable; you've worked hard. But I think my friends and relations might be a little squashed! Now, why don't you two come with us?"

And so Cousin Willoughby took Whiskers and Twitchit, and all his friends and relations, to the most magnificent hole they'd ever seen. The chandeliers were made of gold, the milk came in big earthenware pitchers and the cheese was exclusive Double Gloucester.

"And they lived happily ever after," concluded More-Haste-Less-Speed. "So it does pay to be ready, you see!"

"Yes, great-grandpapa," Take-Your-Time peered out of the sycamore tree. "It's stopped raining now, so I'd better go. Er - can I borrow your umbrella-leaf, great-grandpapa, so I'll be ready if it starts again?"

More-Haste-Less-Speed chuckled. "Not only in school you learn your lessons well," he remarked.

Jesus told a story about ten girls who were going to be bridesmaids at a wedding. They each had to carry lamps, which burned oil in them. Five of the girls took extra oil with them, in case the lamps ran out before the bridegroom arrived: but the other five didn't. The bridegroom *was* a long time, and all the lamps ran out of oil. But while the five girls who had no spare oil had gone to buy some, the bridegroom came, and they were locked out of the wedding.

Jesus said that he would come back again one day, and he wants us to be ready for him.

Whiskers and Twitchit kept their hole clean and tidy for Cousin Willoughby; what should we do to be ready for Jesus?

3

Let's Pretend. . .

It was a very weepy little tortoise who arrived at his great-grandpapa's sycamore tree a few days later, clutching More-Haste-Less-Speed's umbrella-leaf in one paw.

"Thank you," More-Haste-Less-Speed took it. "Now, whatever's the matter with you, my lad? Didn't know there were that many tears in the ocean!"

It took Take-Your-Time quite a while to pluck up courage. "My mother spanked me," he sniffed at last. More-Haste-Less-Speed waited. "I thought I'd pretend the umbrella-leaf was mine, just for fun," said his great-grandson at last. "I was going to give it back, honestly I was! But she was furious. Great-grandpapa, it doesn't really matter that much, does it - not in the Long Run?"

More-Haste-Less-Speed wagged his head from side to side. "You know what they say," he said solemnly. "Sow a thought, reap an action; sow an action, reap a habit! You remember I told you about the day when we'll get our lovely golden shells?"

Take-Your-Time nodded, still sniffing.

"Well, too many bad habits will turn you into the sort of tortoise who wouldn't know what to do with a golden shell if it was handed to him on a plate! So don't you go round pretending things is what they isn't," he finished, with a final wag of his head. "Now, dry your eyes before my bedroom gets flooded, and pass me my keys."

Take-Your-Time handed him the big bunch of sycamore keys and huddled in a corner, very subdued, as his great-grandpapa pulled out a story made up of lots of different colours, and began:

Percival was a lizard: but not just an ordinary lizard - oh no.

Sometimes he called himself Percival, sometimes Percy, or Perce - and sometimes Val, or even Allie. It all depended. He was a sort of greenish colour - sometimes. At other times he was brown, or reddish, or sandy colour, or grey; it all depended. It all depended, you see, on where he happened to be at the time. If he was sitting on the sand, then he would turn a sandy colour; if he was sunning himself on a rock, then he'd turn a sort of rocky grey; if he was slithering across the grass, then he'd be a grassy green colour.

Now, this was all very clever and very convenient. But unfortunately Percival didn't know when to stop, and the other animals used to get very cross with him indeed.

Once, when he was sunning himself on a rock, a grass snake slid past.

"Oh, there's Percival!" he hissed. "Percy, come and play I-spy."

But Percival said "I'm a bump on the rock; and bumps on the rocks can't play I-spy. Goodbye!"

"You're not a bump on the rock, don't be silly," said the grass snake. "Come on!"

But Percival lay as still as a stone and refused to say another word; so the grass snake had to play by himself.

Another time Percival was dozing on the sand when a little crab sidled up to him. "Perce, my sister's got her claw stuck under a rock, and we can't move her! Come and help us pull!"

But Percival said "I am sand. . .

I am sand. . . I am hundreds and thousands of tiny grains of sand piled up to look like a lizard. And sand can't pull. Goodbye!''

"You're mad!" said the crab. "Of course you're not *really* sand, even if you do look like it. Come on!"

But Percival would only shift when the sand around him shifted, and the poor little crab had to find someone else to help her.

Then there was the time when he was resting in the tall grass on the edge of the sand dunes, and a skylark alighted next to him.

"Excuse me," she said very politely. "But that is exactly the place I had in mind for a nest: would you mind very much moving just a little to the left?"

But Percival said "I'm a clump of grass, I'm growing here, I've taken root and I can't move!"

The skylark stared at him in surprise. "Grass?" she said. "Oh no, you're not grass. I'd know a clump of grass anywhere. It's tall and spiky and waves in the wind, and you're little and bumpy and hard!"

Percival was so angry at being called little and hard and bumpy tht he very nearly got up and snapped at her. But then he remembered that grass doesn't snap at people, so he lay very still and refused to speak or move.

So the skylark had to find another place for her nest.

One day Percival found himself in a big cornfield. He couldn't decide whether to be the colour of the corn, or the colour of the earth in between the corn stalks, so in the end he turned himself a sort of mottled gold and brown.

He hadn't been there long when he heard the tramp of heavy boots; they paused a few inches away from him, and a man's voice said "You'd better look lively, Percival, the harvester's coming through here in a minute!"

But Percival said "I'm a mixture of the rich brown earth and the golden corn! Earth and corn can't look lively!"

The man shrugged. "Nor will you be able to any more if you stay there," he said. "But suit yourself!" and the tramp of boots faded in the distance.

Percival lay there very still, thinking how nice it was to be stalks of golden corn, and wondering what a harvester was...

Suddenly there was a most dreadful noise, like a whirring, grinding, roaring earthquake, right behind him. . . And when the noise finally passed on its way, all that was left of Percival was divided between the three bundles of corn that lay where he had lain.

More-Haste-Less-Speed noticed a large tear trickling down his great-grandson's nose. "There, there," he said hastily, folding the story and tucking it into his shell. "Don't worry, lad! That Percival, he was a *particularly* bad pretender, he was; didn't even realise that everyone could see through him! But I'm sure you'll not do it again - so we'll forget all about the umbrella-leaf now: here, have a honeyball!"

Take-Your-Time took the honey-ball, popped it into his mouth and cheered up a little.

"Thank you, great-grandpapa. Are there really lizards like that?"

"Mmm. Called chameleons, they are," said More-Haste-Less-Speed. "But that's a long word for a little tortoise! Now run along, or you'll be in trouble again."

So Take-Your-Time ambled hurriedly off, muttering "Chameleon, chameleon," to himself through his honeyball, to prove that he wasn't as little as all *that...*

It didn't do Percival much good to pretend to be what he wasn't! And lots of people knew that he was only pretending anyway.

Jesus knew when people were only pretending; he knew when people were pretending to believe in him and to love God, his father, and he was very angry with them.

Jesus knows when we're pretending too. And he knows what we're really like! That means that he knows all the nasty things about us that we try to hide and pretend aren't really there.

But the wonderful thing is that, although he knows all the nasty things about us, he still loves us very much, and wants us to be with him in God's family. So we don't *have* to pretend!

4

The Mystery of Christopher

It was really quite late - nearer tea-time than dinner-time - when More-Haste-Less-Speed caught sight of his great-grandson coming down the path. At first, he couldn't make out what Take-Your-Time was doing: he seemed to be bowling something along in front of him with a twig - something that looked rather like a small acorn. But it was the wrong time of year for acorns.

As Take-Your-Time came close to the sycamore tree, More-Haste-Less-Speed realised that it was

the wrong shape for an acorn.
Suddenly, with remarkable speed
for his great age, he snatched the
twig from his great-grandson's
paw, almost knocking him over.

"Ouch! What's the matter,
great-grandpapa?" Take-Your-
Time rubbed his shoulder.

"Where did you find it?" More-Haste-Less-Speed picked up the little pale green and brown object very carefully.

"Sort of hanging from a blade of grass," said Take-Your-Time. "It's quite hard to bowl, it's not smooth enough."

More-Haste-Less-Speed spluttered indignantly. "It's not *meant* for bowling! Bowling indeed!" He turned it over, examining it carefully. "Lucky for you it's all right. Now, sit down and listen!"

Puzzled, Take-Your-Time snuggled into the grass and waited as his great-grandpapa pulled out first his spectacles, then a greyish brown story with a pattern on it:

Christopher was very popular: he was a friendly sort of chap, always ready for a chat and he had an enormous stock of jokes, mostly bad ones. He used to go and help the schoolmistress, Thomasina; he helped her teach arithmetic. Very useful, you see: he just stood there while all the little ones learned to count up to thirteen - 'cos there were thirteen

bits to him, not counting his head, that is. Of course there were other caterpillars around - but somehow everyone agreed that Christopher was the best of the bunch, with his bad jokes and his bright green coat.

So they were all very upset when, one day, Christopher

disappeared. Not just to change his coat, as he did sometimes: no, this time he disappeared and didn't come back. Some of the little ones cried for a few days, until Thomasina found an elderly grasshopper to teach them music instead: but it wasn't the same as having Christopher. And no one ever saw Christopher again.

Until one day, one of the little ones, a young grasshopper called Zizi, arrived at school very excited.

"Zizi's seen Christopher!" the whisper went round.

Thomasina sent for him at once. "Tell us all about it," she commanded.

Zizi rubbed his back legs together nervously while the whole school gathered round. His story was strange, to say the least.

"You see," he began shyly, "I was just hopping along near the hedge in the big buttercup field, when this blade of grass practically knocked me over!"

Thomasina stared at him suspiciously.

"Well, it wasn't the blade of grass, of course," continued Zizi hastily. "It was what was on it. And what was on it was Christopher - I'm sure it was!"

"But you know Christopher well enough," said Thomasina. "Was it or wasn't it?"

"Well, he wasn't *quite* the same," said Zizi. "I think he had a new coat on. And he wasn't quite the right shape, somehow. I thought perhaps he was having difficulty changing his coat - you know how he used to get stuck sometimes - so I asked if he wanted some help. He didn't answer, so I held out a hand to him -" he gulped - "but when I touched him, he was all sticky; it was horrible! So I hopped off to get help."

Thomasina wasn't sure if she believed Zizi or not; but she decided to go along with him to see if Christopher - if it was Christopher - was still there. The whole school wanted to come too, but Thomasina said sternly that they must have their music lesson instead.

Zizi led the way in silence, hoping that Christopher would still be there. He was sure Thomasina didn't believe him.

There was certainly *something* on the clump of grass; Zizi could see that when they were still quite a way away: but it didn't look like the Christopher he'd left.

"In fact," More-Haste-Less-Speed looked over his spectacles at his great-grandson, "it looked exactly like what you've just been bowling down the path."

They stopped right underneath the clump of grass. Zizi fidgeted.

"Well," said Thomasina at last. "Whatever that is, it's certainly not Christopher!" She peered at it. "It looks *very* dead," she added, wrinkling her nose. "Fancy telling me that was Christopher! You ought to be ashamed of yourself; getting all the children excited too." And she marched him back to school.

Zizi hung his head. Certainly whatever it was didn't look like Christopher - hardly at all. But it was the same size - and in exactly the same place - and Zizi had a *feeling*. . . surely Christopher wouldn't just have vanished without saying goodbye to anyone?

And every day Zizi would hop past, just to see. . .

One day, as he approached the clump of grass, a movement

caught his eye. Cautiously he hopped nearer. Something very strange was happening! The pale green, shiny case had started to split - and something was trying to get out!

Zizi watched entranced as, with immense care and delicacy, the creature slowly emerged, kicking and pushing feebly at the case to free itself. Was it - could it be?

Slowly it edged its way from the pale green shell, spun itself a couple of threads and gently hung out its wings to dry. It was the most beautiful butterfly!

For a long time, Zizi couldn't bring himself to speak; but finally he plucked up courage. "Christopher?"

The butterfly half turned towards him and - Zizi was quite certain - winked. "Yes," he said - and it was Christopher's voice right enough - "But don't go telling everyone, they'll never believe you!"

But Zizi couldn't help it; he dashed straight off to school to tell Thomasina and the others. But they didn't believe him - and Zizi had to admit it sounded a bit far-fetched. And when he passed the clump of grass on his way home, there was no sign of the butterfly or the pale green case, and Zizi wondered for a moment if he had been dreaming. But he knew he hadn't, and promised himself that one day he'd find Christopher again.

"Do you mean," Take-Your-Time waved a foot at the acorn-like object he'd been bowling, "that one day a butterfly will come out of *that*?"

More-Haste-Less-Speed nodded. "If it doesn't get used by too many ignorant young tortoises to play skittles or what have you!"

Take-Your-Time fidgeted guiltily.

'Mmm. . . just goes to show," reflected his great-grandpapa, removing his spectacles and wiping them on a leaf. "You can never go by appearances in this world - nor in any other, I don't suppose," he added, "but I wouldn't know about that."

Do you know what happened when Jesus died?

Lots of people saw him die on the Cross, and they saw him buried in a cave with an enormous stone rolled in front of it. But three days later some of his followers said that they had seen him: he was alive again! Most people didn't believe them because it sounded so strange - but it was true, just as it is true that a beautiful butterfly comes out of a plain, hard little case.

And that's not all. When God looks at us, he sees something a little bit like the plain, hard case: we're not very beautiful, nor very good. But God wants to make us into something perfect and lovely, like the butterfly - and he can, if we will give our lives to him.

5

Whisper on the Wind

"I must say, it's good to know spring's back," More-Haste-Less-Speed stretched out his neck and waved his head from side to side.

"How do you know, great-grandpapa?"

More-Haste-Less-Speed looked surprised. "Why, the leaves are uncurling, the celandines and primroses are venturing out, and the cuckoo's been singing fit to bust all day! Don't tell me you haven't noticed."

Take-Your-Time hung his head. "I'm afraid I've been running

errands all morning for Mum;
then I played marbles with Easy-
Does-It, so I haven't really had
time to notice."

"Busy, busy, busy," More-
Haste-Less-Speed waved his front
paws in agitation. "People are too
busy to *live* nowadays! No time to
watch the world growing, to
measure the flowers opening, to
listen to the earth singing!"

Take-Your-Time squirmed. "I've got time to listen to a story, great-grandpapa!"

More-Haste-Less-Speed pretended to sigh. "Pass me the white speckled one," he said, reaching for his spectacles:

There was great excitement among the birds - such a twittering and a chattering, such a fluttering and a flapping you never saw. The King was coming! The great golden eagle himself, so the message went, would be visiting as soon as spring arrived. Immediately all the birds called a conference to decide who should do what. The starlings were in charge - they always talked more than anyone else anyway.

"Larks! We want you to compose a special new chorus in honour of the King; then you will fly up, up, up as high as you can in the sky and sing it for all you're worth!" The larks twittered excitedly and went into a huddle to start composing.

"Cuckoos! You'll provide the entertainment - everyone always laughs at you anyway, so you may as well make yourselves useful for once!" The cuckoos looked indignant, and the eldest cleared his throat angrily; but then he thought better of it. It would mean, after all, that the King would pay a lot of attention to them.

"Finches! Yes, all of you, sisters, cousins, aunts, in-laws! Will you be in charge of tidying up? Everything must be absolutely spotless; not a dead leaf, not a feather, not a flower petal to be left lying around - understood?"

The finches nodded, and fluttered off to assemble their brooms, feather dusters and polish.

Then the starlings summoned all the birds of prey together, and gave them instructions about ordering the banquet.

"And what are *you* going to do?" someone rashly asked the chief starling.

"Us?" he said in surprise. "Why, organise, of course!"

Everyone rushed round, busily doing what he was told - or not, as the case might be. All except old Solomon owl. And he just sat, way up in the branches of a great oak tree, and watched, and watched, and listened and listened.

One day young Chester cuckoo had the cheek to fly up and ask why he wasn't helping. Solomon gave him a long, hard stare, until Chester began to feel quite uncomfortable.

"*I* am minding my *own* business," he said at last. "And I could wish everyone else would do the same. But if you must know," he added, taking pity on Chester, who was very young, "I'm listening to the wind."

Chester would have liked to say something rather rude, but he

didn't dare; so he flew off to tell the starlings instead.

"It's really not right," he complained. "There's all of us, slaving away till we're dead beat, and there's him doing nothing but fluffing out his feathers and 'listening to the wind'. Listening to the wind, indeed!"

And the starlings secretly agreed that if Solomon wouldn't help, then he shouldn't be invited to the banquet.

But a couple of days later, Solomon flew down just as everyone was packing up for the night. "The King will be coming alone," he told the chief of the starlings.

"Alone? But he *can't* be! How do you know?"

"I heard it blowing in the wind," said Solomon, and flapped

back to his tree without another word.

The starlings held a hasty consultation. If the King was really coming alone, they had ordered far too much food and at least half their other preparations were unnecessary. But he couldn't be! Whoever heard of a King travelling without his court?

"And what right's Solomon got, coming and sticking his nose in when he hasn't lifted a finger to help?" added Chester, who was eavesdropping.

"Quite right," agreed the starlings. "Carry on, everyone!"

The next evening, Solomon was back. "Bad news," he said. "The Queen has been seriously hurt in an accident; the King will still come, but he particularly wishes that there shall be no celebrations and that everyone shall be sober and serious."

This time the starlings just laughed at him. "That blew in on the wind too, I suppose?"

Solomon ignored the sarcasm. "You'd be surprised what you can pick up just by listening - but of course you're all too busy rushing round making a noise." And he flew off.

As the great day approached, preparations grew even more frantic. You couldn't see the treetops for feather dusters, nor move for all the stores of food piling up, nor hear yourself think for the cuckoos and larks practising. At last an excited whisper was passed round: "The King is coming!"

The King was coming! Immediately the larks soared high

into the air and began their magnificent new chorus. The finches put away their dusters and formed up in lines. The banquet was hastily laid, and the cuckoos began tumbling around and telling jokes.

But - where was the royal procession?

Walking slowly, eyes to the ground, the gold of his feathers hidden by a dark cloak and quite alone, the King approached. The singing, the tumbling, the jokes all stopped abruptly. The King looked up, and saw them all in their Sunday best, and smelled the great banquet. Then he looked away, and saw Solomon, perched up in his oak tree, watching uncomfortably.

"Solomon," he said, "didn't you tell them?"

"Yes, Your Majesty," said Solomon, "but they were too busy to listen."

"Take me to your house for tea," said the King. "This is too much."

And, as the rest of the birds

crept away, Solomon took the King back to his oak tree.

"So you'd better do some listening as well as some doing," concluded More-Haste-Less-Speed, "or you won't know what you're doing your doing for anyway - or if you're doing it right!"

"Yes, great-grandpapa; great-grandpapa," said Take-Your-Time, "the dandelion clock's striking five, so I'd better do something about going home to bed!"

Sometimes we think that God always wants us to be doing things for him; but we must *listen* to him too, to find out what he is like, and what things he wants us to do.

Jesus once went to have supper with two sisters, Martha and Mary. Martha was busy in the kitchen all the time, getting the food ready, but Mary came and sat at Jesus' feet and listened to what he had to teach her. Martha was angry because she was having to do all the work, but Jesus told her that Mary was right to spend time listening to him.

When we come to pray to God, we must remember not to talk all the time, but to listen too!

6

Slocum's Choice

"You see, you've got to go one way or the other," said More-Haste-Less-Speed. "You can't go both ways at once."

He and Take-Your-Time were standing at the place where the path forked and examining a peculiar arrangement of sticks. Take-Your-Time was always impressed by his great-grandpapa's wisdom.

"But who put the sticks there, great-grandpapa?"

"People," said More-Haste-Less-Speed. "I think the ones they call Boy Scouts: a couple of them go off in front and leave a trail for the rest of them to follow. I overheard some dogs talking about it," he explained. "One of them had been told off for leaving signs too."

Take-Your-Time dangled the sycamore keys.

"In the Long Run," More-Haste-Less-Speed pulled out a long, shiny story, "it matters a good deal which way you go; you just listen!"

He cleared his throat, adjusted his spectacles and began:

This is a true story and it happened to *my* great-grandpapa, Slocum. Good fellow he was; maybe not very quick on the uptake, but none the worse for that. Now, he lived near an ageing rattlesnake, name of Rex. Of course, the likes of us is always a bit wary of rattlesnakes: a snake's a snake, after all - but Rex was one of the best. Never hurt a fly, and had the wisest head for miles.

One day, Slocum had a bit of a problem - family matter, you know - and he plucked up courage to ask Rex's advice. Rex gave a gentle rattle.

"Delighted," he said. "Now, if I were you. . . and that's what The Books would tell you too," he finished. Slocum was most grateful. "Any time," said Rex. "Don't hesitate to ask."

And so, whenever Slocum had a problem, he went to find the rattlesnake, and Rex never let him down.

Then one morning there came a

slithering sound outside Slocum's front door, and the bell rang. Slocum was surprised: he supposed it must be Rex, though he had never called before, and hurried to the door.

Outside lay a snake, certainly; but it was not Rex.

"Good morning, Slocum. May I introduce myself? My name is Addle - at your service."

Slocum gazed at his visitor; he was a palish yellow, with a dark zigzag pattern all down his back, and a sort of V shape behind his head. Very handsome, he was, and Slocum felt honoured to have such a distinguished visitor, and one who spoke so respectfully.

"Pleased to meet you," he said. "What can I do for you?"

"I think it's more a case of what *I* can do for *you*," said Addle. "May I come in?"

Now, a few weeks before, Slocum wouldn't have dared to stay near a snake of any description; but Rex had won his confidence, and he thought Addle must be a friend of his.

"Of course," he held the door open and Addle glided in.

"I understand," Addle coiled himself around a chair, "that you've been visiting your cousin Turtle and lending him money."

Slocum looked surprised. "Well, yes," he said. "I asked Rex, and he pointed out that Turtle had had a lot of bad luck and needed some help to get him on his feet again. But how -"

"How do I know, and what business is it of mine?" interrupted Addle with a charming smile. "It's just that I happen to know that you'll never get the money back; Turtle has no intention of repaying it, and he's been spending it all on boat trips. And you can't really afford it, can you? Take my advice, my friend, and look after yourself instead!''

And Slocum was left gazing at the empty space where Addle had been. Was he right? Perhaps he should stop visiting his cousin and giving him money. Turtle's shell was almost mended now after his accident, and he would soon be able to fend for himself again. . .

It was nearly a week later when there was a rattle outside the door and Slocum opened it to find Rex outside, shaking raindrops from his tail.

"Come in;'' for some reason Slocum felt slightly uncomfortable.

"Just popped in to find out how business was going,'' said Rex.

"Oh, not bad, not bad at all.'' Slocum made and sold tins of shell polish. "Not much money in it, of course, but there you are.''

Rex nodded. "A worthy trade; keep it up. I understand you're not visiting Turtle any more?"

Slocum wriggled. "Well, he's almost better now - and as Addle said, I haven't really got any more money to spare."

"Addle?" Rex whipped round so suddenly that Slocum drew back in alarm. "Addle's been here?"

Slocum nodded. Rex looked very stern. "Slocum, don't ever let him in again - and don't listen to what he says. You can't please both of us; understand?"

Slocum nodded - rather reluctantly. Who was Rex to order him around?

"Turtle's been missing you," added Rex. "And he asked me to give you this," and he handed Slocum a small packet that jingled and, with a final rattle, made his way out.

Slocum didn't even notice Addle glide in; suddenly, there he was.

"Just a thought," he hissed gently. "Not much money in shell polish, is there? Ever thought of doing something else?"

"Oh, I couldn't give up my shell polish," Slocum was indignant. "Besides, Rex would be angry - he told me to keep it up. And I couldn't do anything dishonest."

Addle looked hurt. "Who said anything about dishonest?" he said. "Just one or two bits of jewellery I'd like you to look after for me until I can - er - dispose of them."

Slocum thought. Didn't seem to be much harm in that - and he could make his shell polish at the same time. Besides, Addle was looking at him in an almost - threatening sort of way.

"OK," he said. "And I can sell shell polish too, so Rex will still be pleased."

Addle looked annoyed. "you mustn't let yourself be ordered about by that rattlesnake for the rest of your life," he hissed.

It so happened that Rex was there when Addle arrived later with the jewellery. For a moment Slocum thought there was going to be a furious battle, for hatred gleamed in both snakes' eyes and their tails lashed at the ground. In the end Addle said, with a jerk of his head towards Slocum, "Well, shall we let our friend here choose which of us he will have for adviser? I have your interests at heart, my friend," he added.

"Yes, he must choose," said Rex. "That jewellery's stolen, Slocum; and I have somthing more for you from Turtle. You can't please both of us," he repeated. "Choose!"

More-Haste-Less-Speed fell silent.

"Well," said Take-Your-Time, "Which did he choose?"

"Which would you have chosen?" said his great-grand-papa.

"Rex," said Take-Your-Time. "Except I'd have been afraid of Addle."

"So was my great-grandpapa," said More-Haste-Less-Speed. "But he chose Rex too, and he never regretted it. Addle never left great-grandpapa alone, but they taught him a thing or two, him and Rex!"

Slocum wanted to choose whichever way was easier for him, even if it meant disobeying Rex, who had helped him so much. It *is* tempting, isn't it?

At the very beginning, when God made man, he told him not to eat the fruit of a tree in the middle of the garden of Eden. But then the Devil came and said "Go on, eat it! It won't hurt you, it will make you wise!" So Adam and Eve disobeyed God and ate the fruit.

Ever since then, the Devil has tried to make us do things that are wrong, and it's not always easy to say no.

But we cannot please God and the Devil, just as Slocum couldn't please Addle and Rex. Every time we have to choose between two things, we must make sure we choose the right one: the one God wants, not anyone else!

7

The Revenge of Dolly Moomuch

"Hmm! Not bad, not bad at all!" More-Haste-Less-Speed handed his great-grandson back his end of term report. "Reading: very good progress. . . I'll tell you what," he beckoned Take-Your-Time to come closer and whispered in his ear. "Next time you come, you shall have a story of your very own!"

"Great-grandpapa!" Take-Your-Time couldn't believe his ears. "Really? My own for keeps?" And he jigged excitedly from one foot to the other until More-Haste-

Less-Speed told him to stop it, he was getting dizzy. . .

"Not so hot on maths, though, are you? Let me see. . . 'Take-Your-Time should concentrate more on his sums and less on his neighbours' - what's all that about, then?"

Take-Your-Time stopped jigging and hung his head. "It's Easy-Does-It," he said. "He sits next to me - and he can't do maths either, so he tries to play noughts and crosses on my shell instead, or else writes rude notes and passes them under the desk."

"And you *have* to reply, of course," said his great-grandpapa sarcastically.

"Of course!" Take-Your-Time didn't notice the sarcasm. "What else could I do?"

"Ignore him and get on with

your work?" More-Haste-Less-Speed held up a paw as Take-Your-Time was about to protest. "No, you just listen a minute." And he reached for the sycamore keys, unlocked the bumpy door in his shell and drew out a leaf the colour of very milky chocolate. Take-Your-Time tucked his report back under his shell and settled down to listen.

Daisy and Dolly Moomuch
lived in the corner of an enormous
field; The corner with the old oak

tree and the place where the shady, uncertain little stream decided to become a pool. Daisy and Dolly were the finest Jersey cows in the neighbourhood. Everyone thought so: the farmer, of course; and all the villagers; and the rest of the animals on the farm, even the other cows. And Buzz Off.

His real name was Barnaby Buzz, but when he was little, everyone said "Oh, buzz off!" to him so often that he thought *that* was his real name - and now it was. At least, that was what everyone called him.

Buzz Off thought Daisy and Dolly were beautiful, with their creamy brown coats, enormous brown eyes and twitchy ears. Every day he went to visit them - and he nearly drove them mad.

Buzz, buzz, buzz. . . where was he now? Perched on their noses, in and out of their ears, practically in their eyes. . . and every time they tried to catch him with a flick of their ears or a thwack of their tails, Buzz Off would zip smartly out of reach and make rude noises.

Dolly suffered most. The

minute she heard Buzz Off coming, she would go all of a twitch, and her mind was so full of him that she'd even forget to chew the cud and count the hours until milking time. She twisted and turned, switched and scratched, fretted and fussed, but she only grew more and more exhausted, and Buzz Off enjoyed himself all the more.

"Take it easy, old girl!" Daisy kept saying. "Don't let him upset you so, little mischief not a fraction your size!"

"What's size got to do with it?" grumbled Dolly. "My eyes are running and my ears are sore and he makes me itch all over! I'll get him one of these days, you'll see!"

Daisy shook her head sadly. "Can't spend your life getting your own back on people," she said. "Doesn't do you or them any good - moo!"

"You're just soft," snorted Dolly, turning her back on her sister. "Let everyone walk over you, you would."

Daisy sighed, but said no more.

It was only a few days later when the accident happened. It was such a fine, hot sunny day that Buzz Off had got up early, and made straight for the corner of the field with the oak tree and the pool and Dolly and Daisy. And ever since early milking time, he had been driving them both mad. But while Daisy was resigned and patiently went on grazing and chewing, Dolly got madder and madder and madder.

"I'll - I'll *murder* you, you pesky little pest!" she bellowed. "I'll blow you into the middle of next week! I'll make you into squashed-fly biscuits! Take - that!"

And she took a violent swipe at him with her head.

Unfortunately, she was standing at the edge of the field right next to the new barbed wire fence which the farmer had put up the week before. Her head went straight between the two strands of wire and there she was, stuck fast, not daring to move because of the spikes.

It was a long time before the farmer discovered her there, and by that time Dolly was very frightened and very subdued. Luckily, Buzz Off seemed to have disappeared.

It took the farmer nearly an hour to get her out, because he didn't want to cut his new barbed wire, and Dolly was so scared she always pushed in the wrong direction, and so heavy that he wasn't strong enough to push her back.

"Phew!" said poor Dolly when she was finally free, her lovely coat all damp and ruffled. "I'll never bother with that silly fly again - it's not worth it!"

Daisy licked her sister's nose and nuzzled up to her.

The next morning, when Dolly was feeling better and the two sisters were taking a stroll round the oak tree, Daisy suddenly stopped.

"Look!" she nodded up into the branches of the oak tree.

It had been raining in the night, and the raindrops still shimmered on a big, lacy spider's-web, delicately stretched between two low branches. The spider was busy making fast the last corner of the web to a twig; but it wasn't her that Daisy was looking at.

In the very middle of the web, his legs tied together and bundled up in a ball, lay Buzz Off, very still and very silent.

Daisy and Dolly looked at each other.

"Always gets what's coming to them in the end," remarked Daisy, and Dolly, stretching her poor, stiff neck, had to agree.

"I'd like to see Easy-Does-It in the middle of a spider's web," giggled Take-Your-Time.

More-Haste-Less-Speed glared at him over his spectacles.

"Whatever may or may not be coming to your young friend," he said severely, "is not for you or me to say. But when your next term's report comes out, I want to see 'Maths: excellent'!" He poked Take-Your-Time with his spectacles. "You get my point?"

It's easy to want to get your own back, isn't it?

If somebody 'borrowed' your pencil and didn't give it back, it might make you want to take something of theirs in return!

But Jesus tells us that it would be wrong to do that. He said that we must not pay back one wrong thing with another: we must overcome wrong things with right ones. This means that if someone hurts us in any way, we must not try to hurt them back, but to be kind to them.

This may not always seem fair; but God says that *he* will one day deal with the people who have done wrong things: it is up to him, not to us!

8

The Lake

The next day, Take-Your-Time was up at crack of dawn - or very soon after. His mother couldn't understand it- "In the holidays, too!" she said in amazement.

Take-Your-Time grinned at her, swallowed a hasty breakfast of dandelion leaves washed down with morning dew, and set off at a brisk amble for his great-grand-papa's sycamore tree.

More-Haste-Less-Speed chuckled to himself as he watched Take-Your-Time hurrying down the path.

"No prizes for guessing why you're so keen to see your poor old great-grandpapa, eh?"

"Oh, great-grandpapa!" Take-Your-Time was indignant. "It wasn't just the story - I *like* seeing you! But you hadn't forgotten about the story, had you?" he added anxiously.

More-Haste-Less-Speed winked at his great-grandson and beckoned him inside the sycamore tree. With great ceremony he unlocked a little cupboard in the corner and carefully drew out a large, golden envelope, which he handed to Take-Your-Time.

"Treat it as your most treasured possession," he said solemnly, as Take-Your-Time slowly unfastened the envelope, paws trembling, and pulled out the story. It was perfect: golden brown tinged with red, plucked at the height of autumn before the November rains had a chance to curl its edges or make nasty brown patches on it. . .

"Oh, *thank you*, great-grand-papa!" whispered Take-Your-Time. "Can I read it now?"

"It's your story," replied his great-grandpapa. "Here, draw up some bedding and make yourself comfortable." He pushed some dry grass and leaves over. "Now, you can have a good read while I - er - have a good - er - forty winks. . ."

So Take-Your-Time snuggled into the dusty grass, spread out his story in front of him, and began to read:

Tortoises, as you know, are a calm, easy-going bunch - a lot of stick-in-the-muds, you could say, if you wanted to be unkind. It's a rare thing for a tortoise to get excited - and an even rarer thing for lots of tortoises to get excited all at the same time. So when all the tortoises in the park started chattering and plotting, flapping and pottering round in all directions at once, you could tell that Something Was Up.

It was Tertius, a young tortoise just out of school, who first discovered the green, green grass - "Greener than anything you've ever seen or rolled in," he assured the others, his eyes wide. "And it's not very far - just the other side of the fence at the bottom of the paddock."

Now, the fence at the bottom of the paddock may not have been very far, but no tortoise had ever dared to venture under it; so it was all a great adventure.

One by one the other tortoises had taken it in turns to go with Tertius down to the fence and peer under it at the green, green grass on the other side. And it certainly did look inviting: it sparkled and shimmered in a way that ordinary grass never did, and the colour was so bright that Tertius privately thought that whoever made it must have upset the paint pot all over it.

Tertius was a good organiser, and soon all the tortoises were packing up their belongings and collecting their children ready for the big move.

"When are we going?" said Totty, one of the youngest of Tertius' brothers and sisters.

"Next Friday," said Tertius importantly; and so the whisper went round "We're going on Friday! Are you ready?"

There was just one thing; Totty met the Boy, and of course, she had to tell him all about it. (The Boy was the son of the Lord of the Manor who owned the park and, so he said, all the tortoises.) The Boy was horrified when Totty told him what they were going to do.

"Green grass?" he exclaimed in horror. "That's not green grass, you silly things, that's the reflection of all the trees in the lake!"

"Lake?" Totty was puzzled.

"Water," explained the Boy.

"Oh no," said Totty. "I know what water is - it collects in the hollows of stones, and sometimes you put some out for us in a dish. And it's never green."

The Boy shook his head in despair. "It's not the water that's green, it's the *trees* - if you waited till autumn, the water would turn orange and yellow and brown to match the trees. . . Oh dear, you'll never understand - but you must believe me!" The Boy sounded so upset that Totty thought perhaps she'd better tell Tertius. But Tertius just laughed.

"He doesn't want us to go, that's all," he said. "It will be further for him to come and see us, and to give us water."

"Perhaps he won't come, then," said Totty anxiously. She liked the Boy.

"Oh, we'll manage, even if he doesn't," said Tertius airily.

The next day, which was Tuesday, the Boy came specially to see Tertius. With him he brought a large pan of water, a piece of red paper and a piece of green paper. Then he led Tertius into a patch of sunlight.

"Now, look!" he commanded,

and held first the green paper, then the red, at an angle over the water. The water reflected a patch of green ripples, then a patch of red.

"You see?" said the Boy triumphantly.

"No," said Tertius obstinately. "What's that got to do with grass?"

"Oh, I give up!" The Boy crumpled up the paper in despair. "Here, look at it this way - my father owns this park, right?"

Tertius nodded.

"So he ought to know what's on the other side of the fence, right? And it's water!"

"Chris!"

"Bother," said the Boy. "It must be dinner time. But it's true, Tertius - don't go!"

The next day, and the next the

Boy was back. He talked to several of the other tortoises and told them what he had told Tertius. But they were all so full of the idea of the lovely green grass that they refused to listen to him, and on Thursday evening, when the Boy left to go home, his face was white and very serious.

Early on Friday morning all the tortoises gathered under the big chestnut tree, and formed into a rather ragged procession with Tertius at the head. Everywhere there were excited murmurings and a fussy lady tortoise with a first aid box rushed round issuing everyone with sticking plaster, in case of blisters.

At last they were all ready, and the big move began.

They had practically crossed the paddock before they realised there was a stranger in their midst. He didn't talk to anyone, but took special care to stay very near the front.

"What's your name?" asked Totty, having finally plucked up courage.

"Chris," he replied briefly.

Totty started, and gave him a long stare, but said nothing.

Very soon they reached the fence, and the procession drew to a halt. Everyone gazed at the green, green grass on the other side, glittering in the sunlight. Then they turned and gazed back at their old home, the paddock and the chestnut tree.

Tertius drew a deep breath. "Forward!" he cried at the top of his voice.

"Stop!"

Everyone stared at the stranger

as he stepped under the fence and turned to face them. "I will go first!"

And before the others had recovered from their astonishment, he was standing on the very edge of the green, green grass. Angrily Tertius made a move forward; but Totty came up beside him and laid a paw on his shoulder. "Wait," she said.

For a long moment, the stranger paused on the edge of the grass. Then he took a great stride forward.

There was a loud 'Splash!' and the stranger disappeared.

It was a very subdued procession which straggled back through the paddock, Tertius lagging a good way behind.

In time they forgot about the move that wasn't, and were

content once more with their paddock; except that it was never quite the same without the Boy.

"You didn't tell me it was a sad story, great-grandpapa," Take-Your-Time gave a loud sniff.

More-Haste-Less-Speed opened one eye. "Some of the most important things may be sad. Depends how you look at it, though," he added. "If all our grandfathers and great-grand-fathers had jumped in the lake, you wouldn't be here now! Nor would I, come to that."

Take-Your-Time folded his precious story. "And I'm glad we are, great-grandpapa!"

Who do you think the stranger was?

God is so much greater than we are that it was impossible for us to understand what he was trying to tell us. That's why, at the very first Christmas, God became one of us - a man called Jesus.

And just as the stranger jumped into the lake to save all the other tortoises, so Jesus died on the Cross to save us all from dying; everyone who believes in him will not really die, but will go to live with him in heaven.

In the story, the Boy disappeared and never came back; but Jesus, because he was God's Son, was able to rise from the dead - and he is alive today!

If we ask him, he will come and live in each one of us, and help us to be like him.